This book belongs to

Mrs. Hurd

Meaner than Meanest

by **Kevin Somers**

Illustrated by
Diana Cain Bluthenthal

Hyperion Books for Children

New York

Text copyright © 2001 by Kevin Somers
Illustrations © 2001 by Diana Cain Bluthenthal

Printed in Mexico

FIRST EDITION
1 3 5 7 9 10 8 6 4 2

Library of Congress Cataloging-in-Publication Data
Somers, Kevin.
Meaner than meanest / by Kevin Somers ; illustrated by Diana Cain Bluthenthal.—1st ed.
p. cm.
Summary: An old hag tries to make the most evil creature in the world, but her spell goes wrong and
she ends up with an annoyingly sweet little girl instead.
ISBN 0-7868-0577-3 (trade)
[1. Witches—Fiction. 2. Magic—Fiction. 3. Behavior—Fiction.] I. Bluthenthal, Diana Cain, ill. II. Title.

PZ7.S6962335 Mf 2001
[E]—dc21
00-022557

Visit www.hyperionchildrensbooks.com

To Jen,
one of the strongest people I've ever known!
—K. S.

To Cameron and Kelley,
my two favorite recipes,
and to those who bring out the best in others
—D. C. B.

WOODED
SWAMP

HAG

HOVEL

$\mathcal{S}$ometime ago, somewhere not too far away, there was a wooded swamp.

In this wooded swamp stood a rickety old hovel that seemed to lean toward the moon.

In the hovel, within the wooded swamp, lived an evil old hag who was the second-meanest creature alive.

She was the second-meanest creature only because a cat named
Hisss lived with her, in the hovel, within the wooded swamp. He was the
meanest.

He was so mean, in fact, that the hag could never get anywhere near
him, even at dinnertime.

The cat hated the hag and the hag hated the cat, and that is
just how it had been for as long as either of them could
remember.

They both liked it that way.

One fall day the hag realized that October thirty-first was right around the corner. She wanted it to be the darkest, spookiest, creepiest Halloween ever. But how to make it happen?

"I'll make a mean monster, the meanest," the old crone said to herself. "Yes, that's it! It'll be even meaner than Hisss and uglier than me." She cackled. "I'll make THE MOST EVIL CREATURE IN THE WORLD!"

The hag eagerly went to work. She rifled through her ratty old books until she came across the one she was looking for. It was titled MONSTER RECIPES FOR WITCHES, HAGS, AND MEAN OLD BATS.

From the cellar she got a big old brass pot and half filled it with greasy, slimy sweat from a speckled frog. She slowly cooked it to a simmer.

EYE OF NEWT

SNAILS

SNAKES

SCORPIONS

SPIDERS

Speckled Frog Sweat

SALT

ROTTEN SQUASH

LIZARD INNARDS

PICKLED EGGS

SPINACH SOUP

She added sixteen scrappy scorpions and seventeen sticky spiders.
After that came six slithery snakes and then half a dozen squishy snails.
Oh, what nasty things she put in that pot!

Soon the pot began to foam up higher and higher until it hardened into a cocoon.

For the next several days the hag sat next to the cocoon.
She read it horror stories.

She called it awful names and whispered to herself, "You're going to be even meaner than Hisss and uglier than me!"

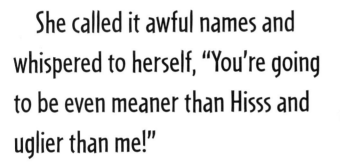

She poked it with a stick, saying "Get mean! Get mean!"

Just as the hag was commanding the cocoon to "Be born and name thyself, evil monster!" Hisss knocked a jar off the table. It was labeled EYE OF NEWT.

"Eye of newt! Eye of newt!" screamed the hag. "How could I have left out the most important part?" But it was too late. The cocoon began to hatch. . . .

Out from the cocoon popped the cutest girl the hag had *never* wanted to meet.

"My name is Daisy!" the girl said with a voice sweeter than honey.

"What have I done!?" cried the hag. She put her head in her hands.

Daisy saw that she was upset and said, "Aw, you look like you need a cup of hot cocoa, or perhaps a hug?"

"A hug? A hug? The last thing I need is a hug!" the hag screamed furiously. She locked Daisy in the next room with Hisss. "Spend some time with the cat. Maybe some of his meanness will rub off on you!"

Later, the hag returned. She was horrified to find Hisss purring in Daisy's arms.

Daisy giggled, saying, "He's really a sweet kitty. I'm going to call him Mr. Fluff!"

The hag showed Daisy and her new friend to the cellar. "Well," the hag cackled. "We'll see how chummy you and Mr. Hugs-and-Kisses are after a few hours together in a damp, dark cellar!"

The hag paced in anger, saying to herself, "That little nonmonster took the hiss out of a perfectly mean cat."

After a few hours, the hag peeked into the cellar. Her face dropped.
Daisy had found some candles and blankets. Warm and cozy, she and
Mr. Fluff were happily playing cards.

"What is this?" the hag demanded.
"We're playing Go fish!" replied Daisy,
adding, "Kitty cats love fish!" The hag left
the cellar, screaming.

The hag tiredly sat in her chair for a while soaking her feet.
"What kind of stupid recipe for a monster makes a little girl when
you forget the eye of newt?"

Around dinnertime, the hag stormed down the cellar stairs, shoved some wormy apples at Daisy, and said, "Choke on these, brat!"

Daisy just smiled, took the apples, and softly said, "Thank you, kind hag."

Later, the hag came back to find Daisy, Mr. Fluff, and three worms playing pinochle. Daisy looked up to say, "Apples are best shared among friends!"

The hag stomped up the cellar stairs, saying, "Let's see how much fun you and all your little critters have, sleeping down there with the rats!" She slammed the cellar door and locked it.

At sunrise, the hag unlocked the cellar door and found herself in the middle of a tea party. It was Daisy, Mr. Fluff, the worms, and three handsome cellar rats. The hag grumbled, "I give up!"

During the next few days the old hag moped around the hovel while Daisy was having fun playing.

She flew kites with Mr. Fluff.

She played freeze tag with the rats.

She made happy drawings with the worms.

The hag couldn't bear it any longer. She locked herself in her room and refused to come out.

On Halloween morning, the hag awoke. At first she was excited by thoughts of the scariest day of the year, but then she remembered. This year a little girl named Daisy was ruining all her hopes of having a truly ghoulish holiday. She decided to stay in bed.

After sunset, there was a knock
at the bedroom door, followed by
a high voice chirping, "Come on,
hag. It's time for trick or treat!"
It was Daisy, of course.

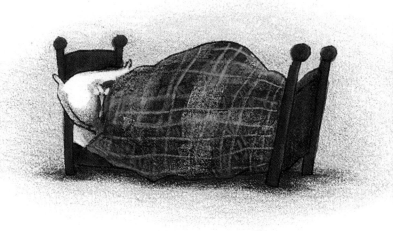

The hag covered her head with her
pillow.

Daisy started again. "Old hag, it's
the witching hour. Please come out
of your dark room."

The hag could not even muster up anger at Daisy's cheerfulness. She dragged herself out of bed and went to the door, grumbling to herself.

She opened the door.

Then something very strange happened. Something that had never happened before in the hag's whole bitter life.

Her face twitched! Her mouth quivered, cracked, and then broke into what can only have been called . . .

a smile.